Lenny the Lion

Short Stories, Games, and Jokes!

Uncle Amon

Published by Hey Sup Bye Publishing

ISBN-13: 978-1535024402
ISBN-10: 1535024402

TABLE OF CONTENTS

Lenny the Lion Wants a Fish

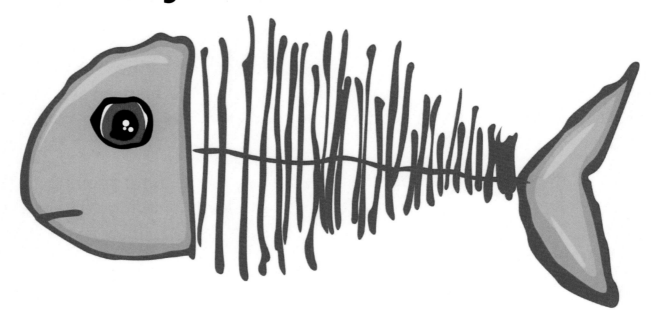

Lenny quietly tiptoed away from his pride. The light of day was beginning to show and before long, the sun would rise above the mountains. Lenny wanted to play down by the river and he knew his parents would never let him do that by himself. He wanted to show them that he was old enough and smart enough and strong enough to take care of himself.

As soon as he was away from the other lions, Lenny ran toward the river. He had been watching other lions catch and eat fish from that river and it looked like fun. It also looked like a good way to get so much to eat that he would not have to share, like when his mother caught the fish or other food. Then all the young lions would have to share what there was and eat what they could. No one ever got enough that way. But today, Lenny was going to fill his stomach so much he would not have to eat again the rest of the day.

Lenny decided he had chosen a good day to catch fish, so he slowly stood up and crept up to the edge of the river. He was still being careful, like his mother had taught him, so that he did not get surprised and hurt by other animals that wanted to eat him.

Lenny stopped at the edge of the river. He bent over and lapped up some water. It was cool and yummy to the taste. He jumped when he heard something moving in the bushes nearby, but then he settled down as he saw a snake slither away with a frog in his mouth.

Lenny was beginning to become afraid. He wanted to hunt and fish like an adult lion and catch his own food. But he was also afraid that he might get hurt and there would be no one from his pride to come and rescue him.

Lenny watched the river again. Now he saw something moving in the water. It looked like a big log, but it was slowly moving toward him. He bent to drink some more water before wading into the river to catch some fish.

Suddenly, the log in the river leaped toward him. The log opened its mouth and hissed at him, showing big teeth. Lenny knew right away it was not a log. It was a crocodile! And it wanted to eat Lenny for its meal.

Lenny quickly ran for his life away from the river. He heard the clomping of the crocodile's big feet in the grass and he heard it snap its big jaws, trying to catch Lenny. But Lenny kept running and did not stop until he was back with his pride again. He ran up to his mother, who was sitting in the sun, grooming his brothers and sisters.

Mother stopped when she saw Lenny running up to her. "Where have you been?" she asked. "I was afraid you might have gone to the river, even though we told you it is dangerous."

Lenny ran over the top of his mother and hid behind her, looking back toward the river. Still trying to catch his breath, he said, "I did go to the river, so I could catch a fish for my meal. It looked safe enough, but a big crocodile jumped out of the water and tried to eat me. I ran and ran all the way back here. I should have listened to you and Father. I promise never to do that again."

"It would have been better if you had listened to me and believed I have enough experience to know how to protect you," Mother said. "But I'm glad you returned safely. We'll all go down to the river later to catch some fish for supper. It's safer when we are all together."

Lenny and the Wildebeest

Lenny strayed away from his pride. He wanted to practice his hunting skills by sneaking up on a smaller animal, then pouncing on it. He didn't want to eat it, he just wanted to practice pouncing. He walked slowly and silently through the tall grass. He listened carefully to the sound of the wind in the grass, to the chirping of the grasshoppers and the croaking of the frogs.

Lenny heard something he could not describe. It sounded like an animal grunting and groaning. Then it would stop for a while, and start up again after a few minutes. Lenny crept in the direction of those sounds to find out what it was.

When he came to the edge of the tall grass, he stopped and listened and waited. He also sniffed the air to help him find out what was making the grunting noises. Between the edge of the tall grass and the edge of the river was a large mud puddle. In the middle of the mud puddle was a wildebeest. It was bigger than Lenny's mother and father. It was stuck in the mud puddle.

While Lenny was watching, the wildebeest started struggling again, trying to get out of the puddle. But it was really stuck.

Lenny walked up to the wildebeest to get a closer look.

When the wildebeest smelled a lion, he was afraid and struggled even harder to get free. But when he saw little Lenny, he stopped struggling to catch his breath.

"How long have you been caught in the mud?" Lenny asked the wildebeest.

The wildebeest panted and snorted to catch its breath after all the struggling. "I have been here since the early morning sun," said the wildebeest.

Lenny had never seen a wildebeest up close before. He knew the older lions hunted and chased them, but he had never spoken to one of them. "Where is your family?" he asked.

"They were afraid of getting caught by lions, so they ran away when I got stuck here."

"How can you get out of the mud?" Lenny asked. He didn't know mud could be deep and dangerous.

The wildebeest blew out a full breath. "I don't know. I have very little strength left to try to climb out," he said.

Lenny looked around the area. He saw a dead tree leaning over the mud puddle and wondered if it might help the stuck wildebeest. He pointed his nose at the tree, then looked back at the wildebeest. "If I can knock that tree into the mud, would it help you climb out?" he asked.

"Yes, it might help me. But why would you want to help me?" asked the confused and tired wildebeest.

"I'm too small to chase after you," Lenny said. "It's no fun chasing something when you know it's too weak to get away. If I help you get free today, maybe you'll be stronger, and I can chase you tomorrow."

The wildebeest laughed at the childish idea. But he wanted to get free, so he said, "If you can help me get free today, then I will help you if you ever need a friend when you get stuck," he said.

Lenny smiled. That sounds good," he said. So Lenny climbed up the dead tree. It was scary because he was afraid the tree would break and make him fall into the mud beside the wildebeest. He carefully bounced on the tree until it broke, then he quickly jumped away from the mud and watched the stuck wildebeest.

The tree fell right in front of the tired wildebeest. It grabbed the tree limbs with his front hooves and slowly climbed out of the mud. Then it turned to look at Lenny. "Thank you, young lion. Do you promise not to chase me, today?" he asked.

Lenny silently nodded his head and the muddy wildebeest quickly ran away before any other dangers could fall upon him.

The Rude Hyenas

One day, Lenny was out playing with three of his brothers and some of the hyena pups. They were wrestling in the grass and chasing each other around large boulders and having a good time.

After a while, Lenny's mother called her cubs to come back home. All three of Lenny's brothers immediately ran to their den to find out what their mother wanted. Lenny didn't want to stop playing, so he stayed with the hyena pups.

Once the other lion cubs were gone, the hyenas started playing rough with Lenny and ganging up on him in their rough play. One of the pups bit Lenny too hard on the back leg and it hurt. But when Lenny started to complain to the pups, they laughed and told him to go back to his mama like the other cubs did.

Lenny didn't understand why they treated him that way and wondered whether he had done something wrong so that they made fun of him and hurt him like they did. But they just called him names and chased him some more—not as part of any game, but to try to hurt him again.

Lenny ran back to his brothers and to his pride and left the hyenas to themselves. If they were going to hurt him, then he didn't want to play with them anyway. As soon as he saw his pride, he ran to them and told them what had happened.

"Why did we have fun together, but as soon as I was alone with the hyenas, they started treating me different and making fun of me?" he asked his mother.

"Whenever you play with your brothers, you play rough without wanting to hurt each other because you are from the same family," she said. "But when you play with young ones from other animal families, they do not love you as much as we do, so they sometimes make fun of you and may even try to hurt you."

"But why?" Lenny asked. "I didn't do anything bad to them," he said. He wanted to understand why they treated him that way.

Mother put her large paw on his shoulder and licked his ears to make him feel better. Then she looked at the wound on his back leg. "It will heal in a few days," she said, softly. "If you want to be treated fairly, then it's better for you to stay with those who love you and will protect you from hunters and other animals. But if you want to go out and meet other animals and play with them, you must understand that they don't love you the way we do and they may sometimes make fun of you. It is wrong, but it is also the way of the jungle."

"Can I try to make it better, so we can all get along with each other?" he asked.

Mother stopped licking his ears. He was all better, now. "Yes dear. I want you to try to make the world better, but you need to understand how it is and why it is that way, first. Watch the other animals and try to be good with them. But don't expect them to always be good to you until they believe you trying to do better, first. Learn to love them and they may learn to love you. Treat others how you want to be treated," she said.

Lenny and the Tortoise

Lenny liked to go out and make new friends. But he didn't like it when other animals ran away from him when he tried to play. Lenny walked into the jungle and saw a group of monkeys. They were happily swinging from the trees and chasing each other.

It looked like good fun, so Lenny tried to join them. As soon as they saw him coming, they all started chattering and screaming and running to the tops of the trees for safety. They were afraid of the lion.

Lenny was confused and hurt. He looked up at the monkeys and said, "I want to play with you. Come down so we can play together."

"No! No! Go away," they cried. We don't want to play with you." Then they started throwing things at Lenny to make him go away.

Lenny slowly walked away from the monkeys. All he wanted to do was play with them. Why wouldn't they let him play? He wondered.

Next, Lenny walked into the grasslands. There, he saw a small herd of gazelle chasing and playing with each other. They were leaping high into the air and bouncing as they ran. Lenny smiled. Surely, they will let him join their play. He ran over to them but before he could talk to them, they saw him and ran away.

Lenny called after them. Please let me play with you," he called. "I just want to play."

One of the younger gazelle turned around and looked at Lenny. "We don't want to play with you," she said. "Go away and leave us alone."

Lenny sadly hung his head and frowned. He could not understand why the other animals would not play with him. He had no one else to play with and wanted a new friend.

Lenny decided to go down by the river and see if any of the animals drinking water would want to be his friend. On the way, he walked through the jungle and he walked through the tall grasslands. He walked over the rocks and finally saw the river ahead of him.

When Lenny looked down at the moving grass in front of him, he saw a tortoise. It was moving slowly toward the river. Lenny stopped and sniffed at the tortoise. Instantly, the tortoise crawled up inside his shell to protect himself.

"Hello," Lenny called to Tortoise. "Anybody home?" He knew that was a stupid thing to say, but he didn't know what else to say.

The tortoise slowly peeked out of his shell. "Ye-es," Tortoise said, slowly. He saw Lenny standing in his path and was afraid to come out of his shell.

Lenny lay down in front of Tortoise with his nose just inches away from the tortoise shell opening. "Hi," said Lenny with a smile. "I'm looking for someone to play with. Will you play with me?"

"I am too slow to play with you," said Tortoise. "If you want a friend to play with, you should find someone the same size, with the same strength and speed as you."

Lenny smiled. "That means I should play with my brothers," he said.

"If you play nice with your brothers, they will play nice with you," said Tortoise. "Then you will never have to search for friends and you will never be bored or lonely."

"Good idea. Thank you, Tortoise for helping me to see that my best friends are really my very own brothers."

Lenny Just Wants Breakfast

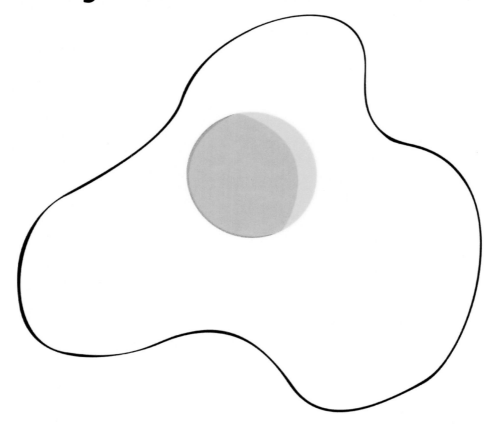

Lenny's mother nuzzled him with her nose. "It's time to get up, she said. He was still tired and the spot he was laying on was warm, so he rolled over and went back to sleep.

Later, Lenny woke up, stretched and yawned real big. He was ready to get up and the day was beginning to get warmer. He slowly walked over to his mother. "I'm hungry," Lenny said. "Where's breakfast?"

His mother smiled, sadly. "I'm sorry, dear. The food is all gone. You wanted to sleep and so your brothers ate all the food."

Lenny looked around at a few bones on the ground. "What am I going to do?" he asked.

"You'll have to wait until we get more food," she replied. "And next time, get out of bed when I tell you it's time to get up."

Lenny's stomach started to grumble. It was empty and he didn't know when he might eat again. So, he decided to go find his own food.

Lenny walked into the high grass, sniffing for something to eat. Suddenly, he heard quick movement and chased after the sounds. He saw a rabbit running away from him through the grass and he started running after it but the rabbit was too fast so Lenny quit.

Lenny walked onto some bare ground with a lot of holes all around. He didn't see any animals, but he waited patiently and finally, several prairie dogs came out of the holes and started looking around.

Lenny jumped up and tried to grab one of them but they also were too fast for him. Lenny was using all of his energy trying to find food and he was getting tired real fast. He took a deep breath and decided to return home without eating. He hoped there was going to be some food for him for supper.

When he got home, he waited and waited and waited for either his father or mother to bring back some food for their children. Finally, both his parents returned but neither of them had any food.

"What will we eat tonight," the cubs all asked at the same time.

Father sadly hung his head, knowing his children would cry without food to eat. "I'm sorry," he apologized. "Maybe the hunting will be better tomorrow. I will get up early and go see what I can find."

So Lenny went to bed with an empty stomach. He did not sleep well, because he tossed and turned and dreamed about food.

In the morning, when Lenny's mother woke up her children, she said, "Boys, it's time for breakfast."

Lenny instantly jumped out of bed and ran to where his father was standing. He had brought food back for the entire family. Lenny looked up at his mother. "I am sorry I didn't listen to you yesterday, when you told me to get up to eat. I promise to listen to you from now on," he said.

Lenny's mother smiled and licked his ears to let him know that she loved him.

Funny Jokes

Q: What do you call a lion on the copy machine?

A: Copy cat!

Q: What happened when the lion ate the comedian?

A: He felt funny!

Q: What is the difference between a lion and a tiger?

A: The tiger has the mane part missing!

Q: Why was the lion-tamer given a ticket?

A: He parked on the yellow lion!

Q: What do you call a show full of lions?

A: Mane event!

Q: Why didn't the lion eat the police officer?

A: He was undercover!

Q: What was the lion's favorite snack?

A: Chocolate chimp cookies!

Q: Why do lions eat raw food?

A: They don't know how to cook!

Q: What day do lions eat people?

A: Chewsday!

Q: What do you get when you cross a lion with a snowman?

A: Frostbite!

Q: What do you call a lion with the chicken pox?

A: A dotted lion!

Q: Why do lions always lose at games?

A: Because they play with cheetahs!

Games and Puzzles

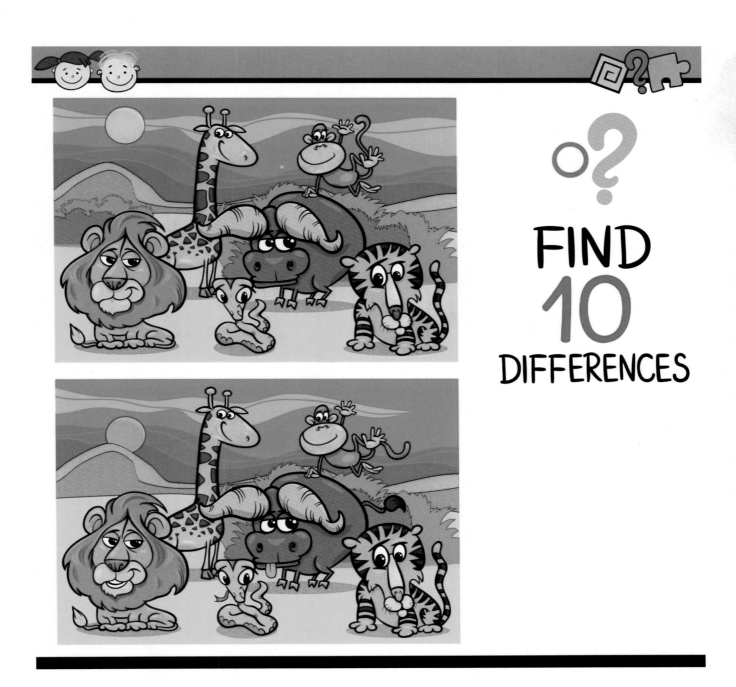

FIND **10** DIFFERENCES

Maze #1

Maze #2

Maze #3

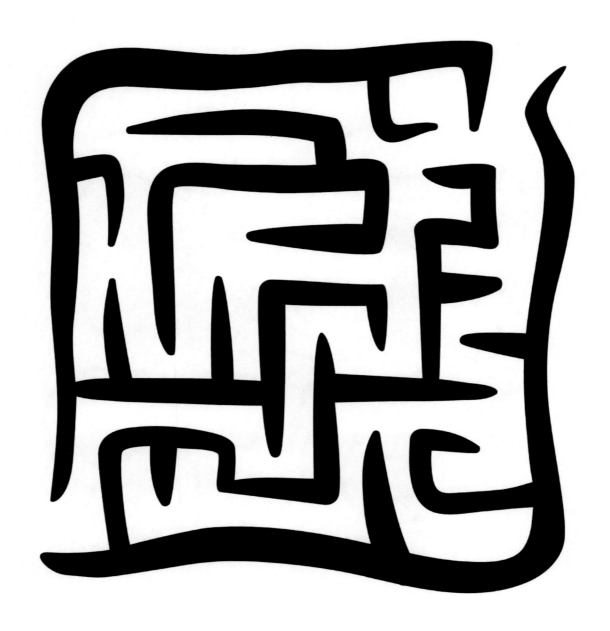

Maze #4

Game and Puzzle Solutions

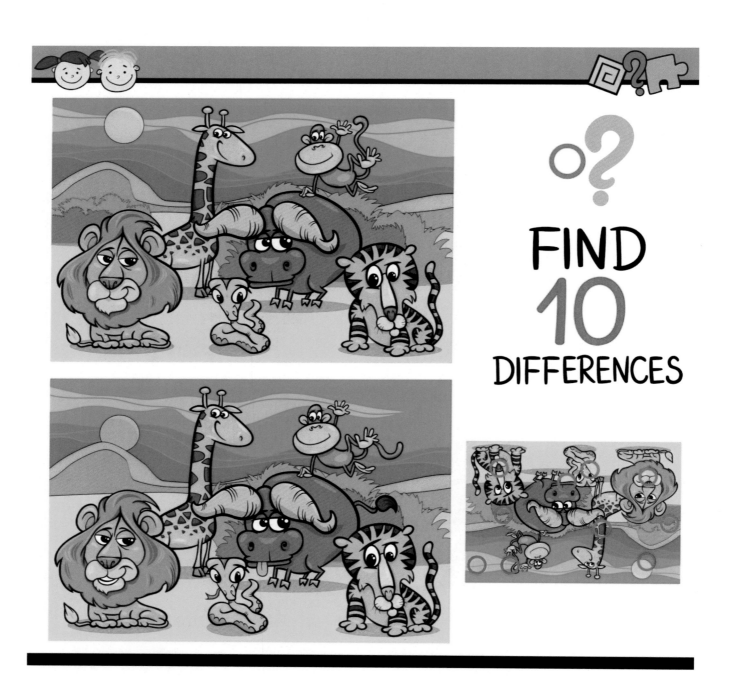

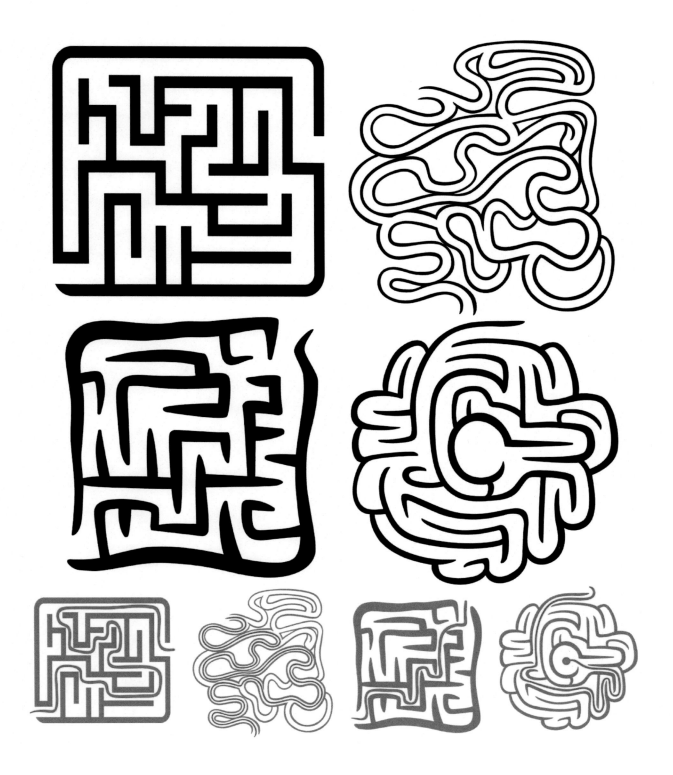

ABOUT THE AUTHOR

Uncle Amon began his career with a vision. It was to influence and create a positive change in the world through children's books by sharing fun and inspiring stories. Whether it is an important lesson or just creating laughs, Uncle Amon provides insightful stories that are sure to bring a smile to your face! His unique style and creativity stand out from other children's book authors, because he uses real life experiences to tell a tale of imagination and adventure.

"I always shoot for the moon. And if I miss? I'll land in the stars."
-Uncle Amon

55654790R00020

Made in the USA
San Bernardino, CA
05 November 2017